THE ADVENTURES OF
MOLLY

By

Mary Nevins

Eloquent Books

New York, New York

Eloquent Books
An imprint of AEG Publishing Group
845 Third Avenue, 6th Floor – 6016
New York, NY 10022
www.eloquentbooks.com

ISBN: 978-1-60693-919-2 / 1-60693-919-X

Printed in the United States of America

This book is dedicated to the memory of my son Damon
who passed in 2006

Table of Contents

Acknowledgements

Illustrations: by Mary Nevins

Introduction

"This is a story of a young girl named Molly, who discovers through her own inquisitiveness her first experience with nature and its surroundings. She is helped by supportive parents along with her childhood pet Labrador named Kelly.

In her first adventure, Molly finds herself befriending a small robin that she encounters in her garden, one cold frosty morning, whilst out playing ball with Kelly.

Molly has an idea to help the robin by putting food out for it to eat and with the help of her parents, they erect a bird table in her garden to help feed the birds through the cold winter months.

Join Molly now as she sets about her task and discover for yourself how rewarding it can be to provide support for the local wildlife.

Frosty Morning

It was not cold enough for ice to form on Molly's bedroom window, but a frost was on the ground in the little garden where Molly played with her toys during the day.

"Molly," called Mummy from downstairs, "your breakfast is on the table."

"Mummy, Mummy," cried Molly, "Jack Frost has been in the garden, can I play outside?" asked Molly.

"When you have eaten your breakfast," replied Mummy, "but you have to wrap up warm."

So, after breakfast Molly put on her warm clothes and her new red woollen hat and gloves she had been given a few days before for her 4th birthday. "Can Kelly play outside with me?" asked Molly. Kelly, was the family's pet black Labrador who could not refuse an invitation to play with Molly and the ball in the garden.

"I think Kelly would like that," replied Mummy, seeing how Kelly's tail was wagging at the thought of being outside.

Molly had to make sure that the garden gate was closed so that Kelly could not run out into the road where the traffic was.

When Molly and Kelly went into the garden, there on the garden fence was a robin. Molly knew it was a robin because she had been given a new book about a robin as a present. Molly thought it would fly away when it saw them, but it sat there singing in the cold frosty air.

Later when Molly and Kelly had gone inside the house Molly asked her Mummy what it was that robins ate. Mummy said that when she was a small girl she knew one that ate dried fruit and nuts.

"Where did you put this food, in the tree?" asked Molly.

Her Mummy laughed, "No, we put these on a bird table that we had in our garden."

"Can we have a bird table Mummy?" asked Molly eagerly.

"Let's see if we can find one at the garden centre when we go shopping this afternoon," replied Mummy.

The Bird Table

Molly and Mummy went shopping into the big town in the afternoon after they had lunch.

On the way back from town, Molly and Mummy stopped off at the garden centre to see if there was a bird table for them to buy and take home with them.

Molly was able to choose one that she liked, which was quite tall and had a small roof on top.

Molly was so excited she wanted Mummy to put into the garden straightaway.

"Let's wait until Daddy comes home at teatime and then we can decide where to put it," said Mummy. "It has to have a hole dug into the ground to put it into so that it doesn't blow over should it become windy."

Molly felt that that afternoon was the longest afternoon she had ever known.

When Daddy came home at teatime, Molly's excitement increased even more. "Daddy," asked Molly, "will you please plant the bird table tonight so that my robin can feed from it in the morning?"

"I shall dig a hole for it next to the fence where you saw the robin this morning," replied Daddy.

"Oh goody," said Molly, "I do hope my robin comes back in the morning."

Daddy planted the bird table where Molly could easily see it from her bedroom window before Molly went to bed that night. She was so excited she had to read her robin book once more before she went to sleep that night.

Feeding Time

The next morning Molly jumped out of bed as quickly as she could and went to look out of her bedroom window. There she could see her new bird table next to the fence ready for her to put out the food for her robin.

She dashed downstairs and asked if she could take some food out to the bird table. "Mummy, Mummy, can I please take some food out for my robin?"

Mummy went to her cupboard where she kept her baking ingredients and found some currents, sultanas and some sunflower seeds.   "I think that this should be enough for the moment," said Mummy.

Molly was so excited she asked if she could take the food out before she was dressed.

She was allowed into the garden with her pyjamas and dressing gown and even only slippers on her feet.

Molly carefully carried out the fruit and nuts that she had put on to two old saucers from her Mummy's cupboard. She carefully put each saucer on the bird table for her robin to feed from.

Then Molly went back into the house and watched from her bedroom window for her robin to come and eat.

It seemed a long time to Molly before she saw it and tried very hard not to shout for her Mummy to see it in case the robin flew away.

'He's 'my robin' Molly thought 'and he will feed from my table everyday.'

Soon other birds came to Molly's bird table to eat the food, but Mummy and Daddy always made sure that there was enough for Molly's robin.

Even when the snowy weather came Molly always put food on the bird table. There were many different birds over the winter, but the favourite of all the birds for Molly, was 'her robin'.

The End

Printed in the United States
1449LVUK00001B